D0573616

DRAWING MANGA™
MONSTERS

Peter Gray

The Rosen Publishing Group's
PowerPlus Books™
New York

Published in 2006 by The Rosen Publishing Group,
Inc.
29 East 21st Street, New York, NY 10010

Copyright © 2006 Arcturus Publishing Limited/
Peter Gray

First Edition

Editor: Alex Woolf
Designer: Jane Hawkins
Artwork: Peter Gray
Digital coloring: David Stevenson

Library of Congress Cataloging-in-Publication Data
Gray, Peter C., 1969-
Monsters / Peter Gray.— 1st ed.
p. cm. — (Drawing Manga)
Includes index.
ISBN 1-4042-3331-8 (library binding)
1. Monsters in art—Juvenile literature. 2. Comic
books, strips, etc.—Japan—Technique—Juvenile
literature. 3. Cartooning—Technique—Juvenile
literature. I. Title. II. Series.
NC1764.8.M65G73 2006
741.5—dc22
2005011759

Manufactured in United States of America

Contents

Introduction

Manga now features in a huge range of magazines, computer games, and graphic novels. It is one of the most popular drawing styles in the world today, especially among comic-book fans.

Although the main characters of manga comics and animes (the Japanese word for animations) are usually human, they are often forced to confront a variety of beasts and monsters, from werewolves to aliens. It's these weird and often scary creatures that we'll be focusing on in this book.

In this book you'll find a wealth of exercises to get you started on drawing in the manga style. There are easy-to-follow steps for you to create a range of monstrous characters, and you'll also find examples to help you develop your own cast of amazing beings.

The most important skill for any aspiring manga artist to develop is the ability to draw, and this will only come about if you keep practicing. Your efforts will pay off eventually, and you will notice how much more inventive and interesting your drawings become.

Salaman

To look at Salaman, it is easy to assume that he is half human, half salamander, but this is not the case. Imagine a world where amphibians are the dominant species. Salaman is from such a world, far from our own planet.

He is a peace-loving vegetarian (except for his weakness for juicy flies and bugs) and retains many amphibious traits, being equally at home in water and on dry land. Look out for Salaman's suggestions and observations throughout this book. They are bound to be insightful.

Materials

Pencils are graded according to their hardness. Number-three pencils are the hardest. These pencils will make the lightest lines. Number-one pencils are softer and will make the darkest lines. Most general-purpose pencils like the ones you use at home or school are graded number two. For the exercises in this book, it will help you to use a hard pencil, like a number three, for sketching light guidelines and a soft pencil for making the final lines of each of your drawings distinct. If you can, use a number-two mechanical pencil to produce a constant fine line for your final image. If your pencils aren't mechanical, they'll need sharpening regularly.

You'll need an eraser too, since you'll have to sketch a lot of rough lines to get your drawing right and you'll want to get rid of those lines once you have a drawing you're happy with. Keep your eraser as clean as possible.

When it comes to coloring, colored pencils are easiest to use. You might want to start with them and then move on to felt-tip pens and watercolor paints when you have developed your skills further. Photocopier paper is fine for most of the drawings you will do in this book. You might want to buy thicker paper if you plan to work with paints, though. This is so the paper won't tear when it gets wet.

Hybrids

Manga monsters are often created from a combination of the features of different animals. This section includes some ideas for inventing such hybrid animals.

The manga dragon we'll draw over the next few pages is a combination of several different animals. Look at the finished picture of the dragon on page 9, then study the pictures on this page so you can get an idea of where its different parts came from.

Lion, Snake, and Crocodile

The manga dragon has a face similar to that of a traditional Japanese-style lion. Its body and head shape are like a snake's, and its limbs sit like those of a crocodile. It has features of other animals, too. It has the antlers of a deer, the whiskers of a catfish, and the mane of a horse. Its feet are a mixture of human hands and an eagle's claws.

Japanese Dragon

This is quite a sophisticated picture, so take your time with each step.

Step 1
Copy the head shape as shown, then add a long, curvy tube for the body. Later you can erase the lines that make up the sections you wouldn't be able to see since they lie underneath other sections.

Step 2
Add the bones of the four limbs and copy the frameworks for the hands. They are shaped to give the impression that the beast is ready to lash out at any moment.

Step 3
Draw the outline for the flesh around the bones. The lines you drew across the finger bones in the last stage should help you see where the joints are so you can curve your outline around these.

Step 4
Let's leave the body for now and concentrate on the head. First, block in the main shapes—the eyes, nose, jaw, ears, and antlers.

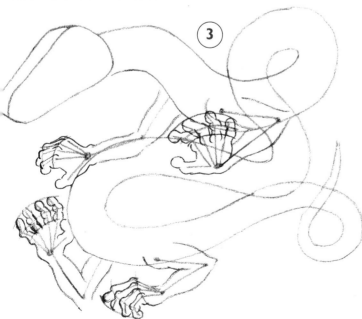

Step 5
Use jagged lines for the fur and teeth. Two curves on the antlers will mark where the skin finishes. Don't forget the tiny pupils and the long, curved whiskers.

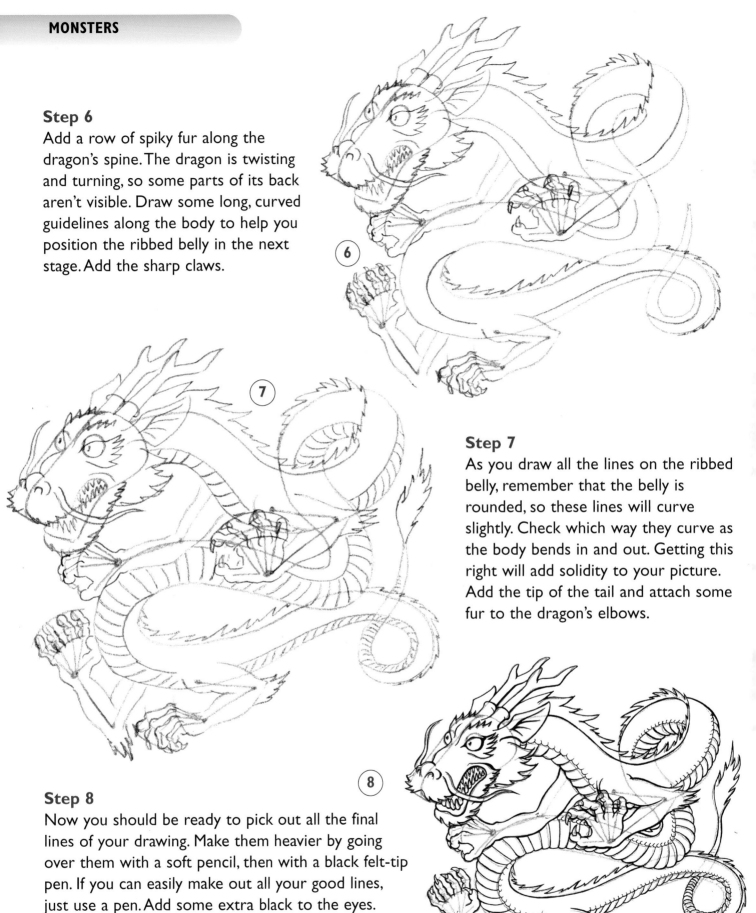

Step 6

Add a row of spiky fur along the dragon's spine. The dragon is twisting and turning, so some parts of its back aren't visible. Draw some long, curved guidelines along the body to help you position the ribbed belly in the next stage. Add the sharp claws.

Step 7

As you draw all the lines on the ribbed belly, remember that the belly is rounded, so these lines will curve slightly. Check which way they curve as the body bends in and out. Getting this right will add solidity to your picture. Add the tip of the tail and attach some fur to the dragon's elbows.

Step 8

Now you should be ready to pick out all the final lines of your drawing. Make them heavier by going over them with a soft pencil, then with a black felt-tip pen. If you can easily make out all your good lines, just use a pen. Add some extra black to the eyes.

Step 9

When the ink is dry, erase all your pencil lines. Now you can decide on a color scheme. Notice that the colors used for the fur make it resemble flames. The inside of the mouth is black to help highlight the ferocious teeth. Don't forget to leave a circle of white on each eye.

More Hybrids

As you get more experienced at drawing animals, you can start to put more of your own ideas into your work. Try creating your own hybrid creatures by mixing the features of different animals. Here are a couple of examples to give you some ideas.

1 This species mixes the features and poses of a crane, horse, and crocodile. Each new creature can be the starting point for a new manga adventure. Be creative as you create your new manga creatures!

2 This new creation has the head shape of a bulldog. A bird's beak takes the place of a nose. The body and pose are similar to a bear's, but the legs are short to help make the character look cute.

Here are some more animal pictures for you to work from to make up some new manga hybrids of your own. Try changing the proportions of the features. Draw the limbs of one animal in a pose you would usually associate with another creature. Practice drawing different-sized creatures. Some might be fierce, some cute, some weird.

Humanoids

Monsters based on humans are known as humanoids. To create them you need to know how to construct the heads and bodies of humans, so as a starting point we'll go through the basic stages of drawing manga males and females. Once you've mastered drawing the humanoids in this section, you'll be able to concoct a tribe of your own fierce and powerful manga beings.

Human Head—Male

This is the head of a teenage manga character, Duke, from a three-quarter viewpoint. He's our starting point for exploring humanoids.

Step 1
To create the framework of the head, start with a rough circle and add a vertical guideline to mark the center of the face. The horizontal guideline comes halfway down the whole head shape. Add a line for the mouth.

Step 2
From this angle, the iris of the eye on the left is smaller and more oval-shaped than the one on the right. It also sits closer to the vertical guideline. Add the outlines of the hair, ear, and neck.

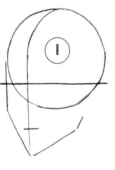

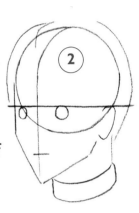

Step 3
Work on the facial features and make the jawline more angular.

Step 4
The angular hair falls from a center part, and there is a bright, circular highlight on each eye.

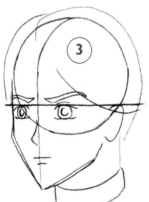

Step 5
Go over the good lines of your picture in heavy pencil, then in pen.

Step 6
Once the ink is dry, erase all your pencil lines and add the color.

Step 7

Next try drawing Duke's head from the front and side. Break it down into steps again, thinking how the skull shape and features will alter with a change of viewpoint.

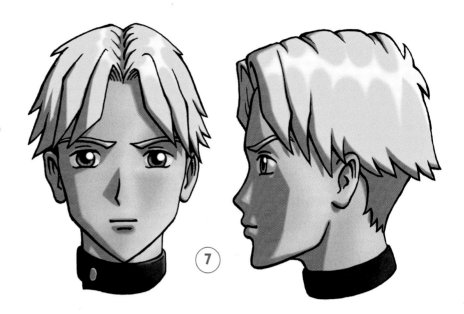

Male Mutations

Once you've practiced drawing a human head, you can alter the features to transform it into whatever mutant you want. Compare each of these pictures with the front view of Duke to see how they differ.

1 Ape boy

Short tufty hair, thick eyebrows, protruding cheekbones, dark eyes, and crease lines that show the wrinkled skin, all work together to give an ape-like appearance.

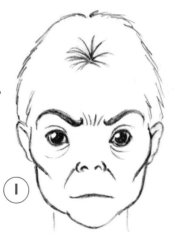

2 Lion boy

The hair here has been styled to resemble a lion's mane. A rough edge has been added to the jawline to imply fur. Fur has also been added to the ears, which are high up on the head. The eyes point down toward a wide nose and mouth.

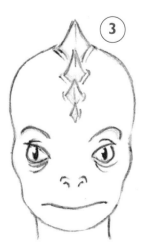

3 Lizard boy

The rounded head shape here is accentuated by a lack of hair. The bony spikes on top of the head, the protruding eyeballs, the nostrils, and the thin, wide mouth complete the look.

4 Bird boy

These large round eyes resemble an owl's. The hair is shaped to look like feathers, and the nose takes the shape of a beak. Notice that eyelashes have been added. These are rare on male human manga characters.

Human Head—Female

This is the head of a teenage manga girl called Daisy. She is about the same age as the male character Duke (see page 12). Manga girls and women nearly always have much larger eyes than do manga males.

Different angles

The easiest way to draw Daisy's head is from the front. Keep in mind, though, manga characters are always on the move, so you'll need to be able to draw them from all sorts of different angles. Try copying these different views of Daisy's head. Some guidelines have been added to the pictures to help you see how they work three dimensionally.

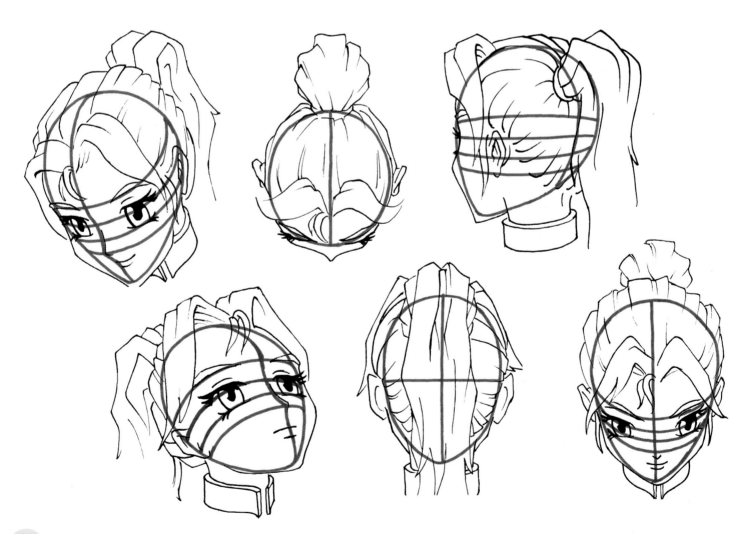

Female Mutations

We can mix up Daisy's features with those of various animals to make new humanoids.

1 Bear girl
Rounded ears that sit high up on the head, a clear hairline around the face, and a nose that takes the shape of a snout all give Daisy a bearlike look. Large, round eyes and short, tufty hair complete the effect.

2 Fish girl
To create an aquatic look, sweep the hair up into a point, add scales to the ears, and draw large round eyes that sit far apart. Notice the distinctive shape of the mouth, too.

3 Monkey girl
Compare this picture with that of the ape boy on page 13. The eyes are slightly bigger, as manga girls' eyes tend to be, and the hair is longer but still tufty.

4 Sheep girl
A matted hairstyle and long curly horns easily identify the animal here. The look is improved by sharply angled eyes and eyebrows.

5–6 Robot girl
Most manga robots are human-based, too. Here are a couple of different styles based on Daisy's face. See what other variations you can come up with.

Centaur

One of the simplest ways of combining human and animal body forms is to attach the top or bottom half of a human to the opposite half of an animal. One creature that takes this form is the centaur, which has featured in stories for thousands of years. It has the head and torso of a man attached to the body of a horse.

Step 1
Since this figure involves drawing two different species, it's best to concentrate on one creature at a time. Start by drawing the human half as shown. The chest takes the shape of an oval with a chunk cut out to show the edge of the ribcage. The oval is tilted to show that the chest is being thrust forward.

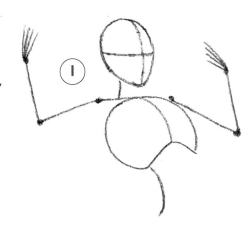

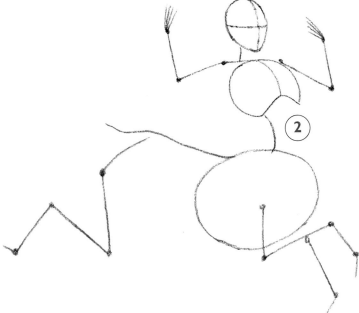

Step 2
Now for the horse. Draw a large oval where the man's hips would normally sit to form the horse's ribcage. Add the horse's backbone and leg bones.

Step 3
Start drawing the outline shape of the flesh and muscle around the bone structure. Notice the deep curve of the horse's underbelly and the strong muscles around the upper arms of the human and the hind legs of the horse. Draw the guide for the remaining leg.

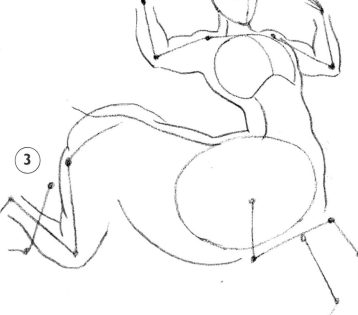

Step 4

Work on the legs and hooves. Notice how the outline curves out around the joints.

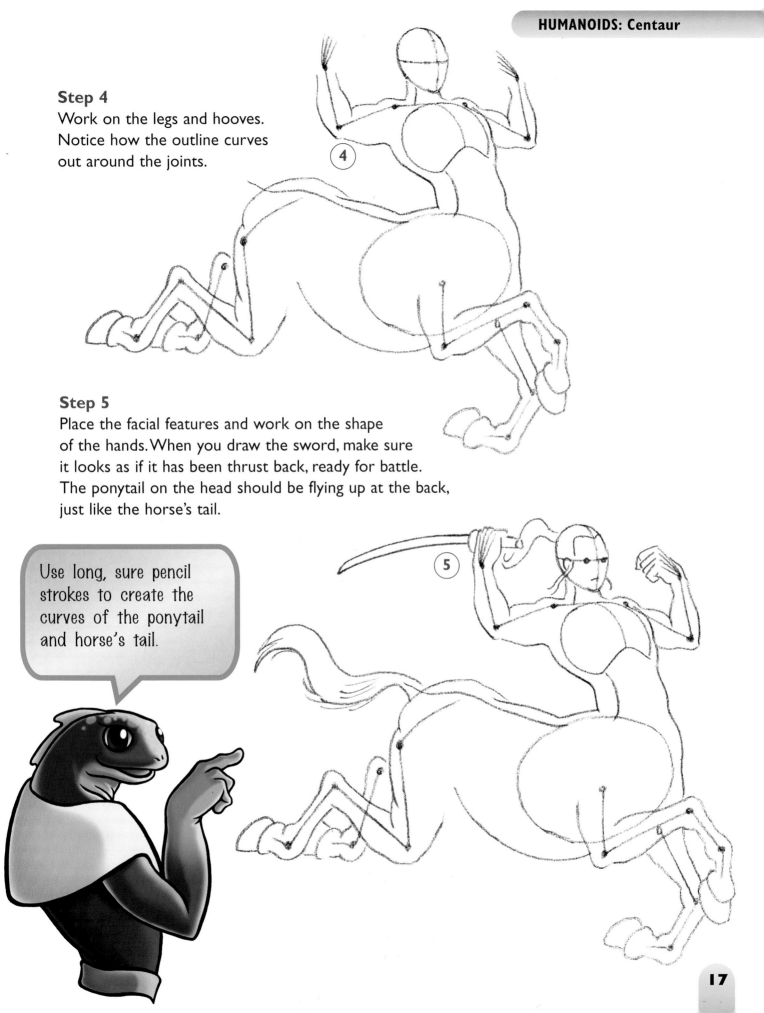

Step 5

Place the facial features and work on the shape of the hands. When you draw the sword, make sure it looks as if it has been thrust back, ready for battle. The ponytail on the head should be flying up at the back, just like the horse's tail.

Use long, sure pencil strokes to create the curves of the ponytail and horse's tail.

Step 6

Add some more detail to the facial features. Make the centaur's jawline more angular and draw lots of little lines on the upper body to define the muscle. A few more curves on the body of the horse will add more definition to the muscle and bone here, too. The lines on the hair help show the direction in which it is flowing.

Step 7

Pick out the good lines of your sketch and go over them with a soft pencil to produce your final picture. Next go over all your final lines again using a black felt-tip pen. Shade in the eyes, leaving a tiny circle of white on each one.

Step 8

Erase all the pencil lines that formed your centaur's skeleton framework, then add the color. This centaur has a zebra's body. His hair is black to match his tail.

Werewolf

The characteristics of a wolf and a man are blended together here so that every feature and body part has the flavor of both species.

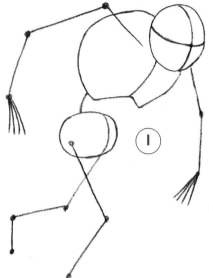

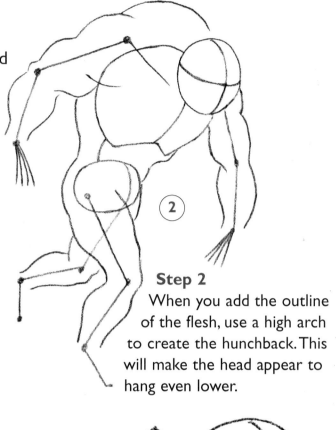

Step 1
Copy the skeleton framework as shown. The angle of the head and oversized chest is crucial to the beast's overall stance. The short legs make the body appear even heavier.

Step 2
When you add the outline of the flesh, use a high arch to create the hunchback. This will make the head appear to hang even lower.

Step 3
Now work on the head. The ears should be pointed and the eyes small. The beast has a long snout and square jawline. Add two rough triangle shapes to the sides of the face for the fur here.

Step 4
Draw the mouth open to display the teeth. Work on the lines forming the hair, including the bushy eyebrows and chin.

Step 5
Add the hands and feet, including the sharp, curved claws. Copy all the curves that define the chest and stomach muscles. Now use some zigzag lines along the beast's back and elsewhere to show the rough texture of the fur. Don't overdo this, since you want the body to retain a human appearance, too.

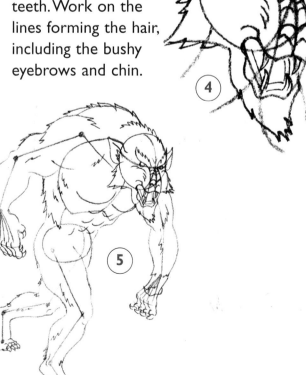

⑥

Step 6

Go over all the final lines of your drawing in heavy pencil, or go straight to ink if you feel confident enough. When the ink is dry, erase all the pencil marks. Shade around the eyes to make the character look more sinister, then apply the color. Notice how the shadows work to make the beast more imposing. The yellow eyes add to the creature's unfriendly appearance.

Alien Project

In this project we will create an alien character from the very first ideas to the finished artwork. The great thing about creating alien characters is that there are no rules. Alien bodies can behave in any way you want them to and have any number of unusual qualities.

Creating an Alien

There's no particular route to creating new characters. Each character evolves in its own way through many stages of drawing. When you aren't sure what you want to draw, there's nothing more daunting than a blank sheet of paper.

1 Doodling
A good way to get started is to give yourself a problem to solve. Take a pencil and some scrap paper and lightly draw a squiggle.

2 Imagining
Looking at your squiggle from different angles, try to make out a face or body hidden among the lines. Draw directly onto your squiggle to develop what you see. This squiggle might make you think of a birdlike form.

3 Shaping ideas
After repeating this process several times, you'll start to get inspiration for the kind of alien you want to create. Insectlike and crablike qualities might work well for an alien creature.

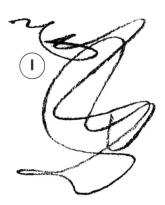

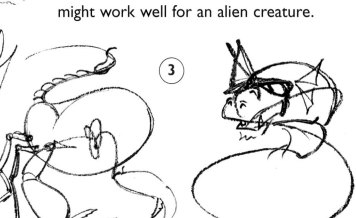

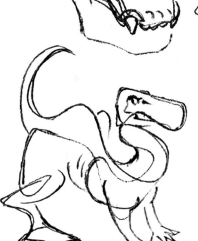

Seeking Inspiration

Once you arrive at the kind of look you want to achieve, you can turn to your sketchbooks for further inspiration. All the examples shown were done during our artist's trip to a natural history museum. Including features based on those found in the natural world can help to make your creatures look believable.

For more inspiration, try dipping the tip of a large brush into some ink and dripping splotches onto some scrap paper to see what kinds of creatures emerge.

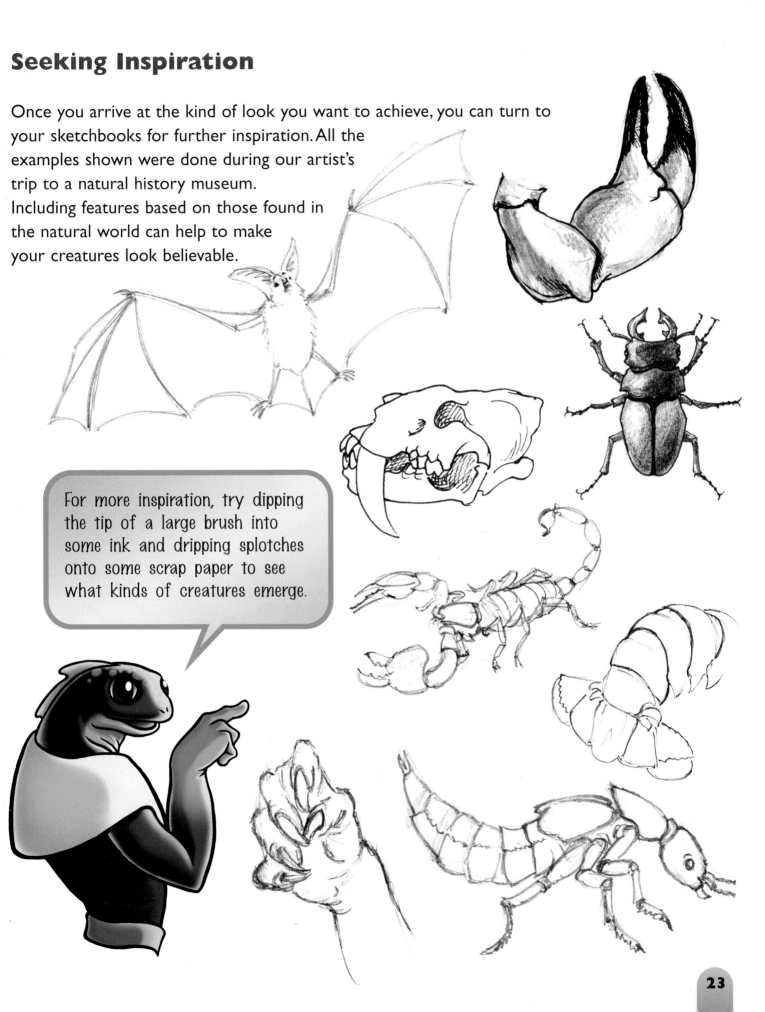

Sketching the Alien

Working from rough doodles and sketchbooks, you can start to develop some alien life-forms. Gradually a character starts to evolve, and each picture will take you one step closer to creating a character you are happy with. Our artist wanted his alien to be fearsome yet graceful and appealing.

If you visit a natural history museum, take a sketchbook with you and draw any animal features that appeal to you. Look at pictures in wildlife books or on the Internet.

Developing the Alien

1 Color sketch

Roughly adding some color to a favorite design can help the artist visualize how a finished version might look. This one is almost there, but it could still be made to look more scary and otherworldly.

2 The pose

For a start, it needs a more dynamic pose. Drawing the skeleton framework of a human allows you to see if a pose will work.

3 Design changes

During the process of sketching your alien in its new pose, continue to develop its body features.

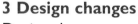

4 The final sketch

As you produce a final sketch, further refine the details and proportions. You could continue to change elements, but at some point you have to settle on a final design. You are now ready to ink and color your final picture. On pages 26–27, we are going to draw the alien shown in Step 4.

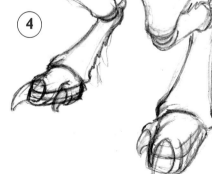

Drawing the Alien

Here are the steps to making a precise drawing of the final alien character on the previous page.

Step 1
Although this
alien's overall body
shape is quite human in form,
there are some vital differences in the
make-up of its skeleton. The outline for the head
is triangular, and there is an extra joint in the neck
to make this longer and more mobile. Notice the
dramatic arch of the spine, too. The chest oval is
much larger than the oval for the hips.

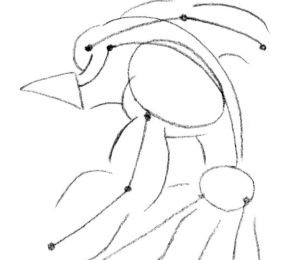

Step 2
Place the arm bones and
joints as shown. For clarity, one
arm is drawn as if it isn't
connected to the body. Notice
how the legs differ from a
human's. The section
between the knee
and ankle is short and the
ankles sit high up.

Step 3
Add the main parts of the body outline
as shown. The body is made up of lots of
separate segments.

Step 4

Fill in the gaps of your alien's body outline. Work on the shape of the head, too. The hands resemble a human's, while the feet are more like an animal's hooves.

Step 5

Start to define the features. Draw in the flesh of the fingers, work on the shape around the hips and limb joints, and add lines to the jaw.

Step 6

Now it's time to add some of the more lethal parts, like the giant fangs and claws and the sharp blade of the weapon. Place the eye at this stage. Work on all the segments running down the spine and the plates that form a shell to protect the creature's back and hips.

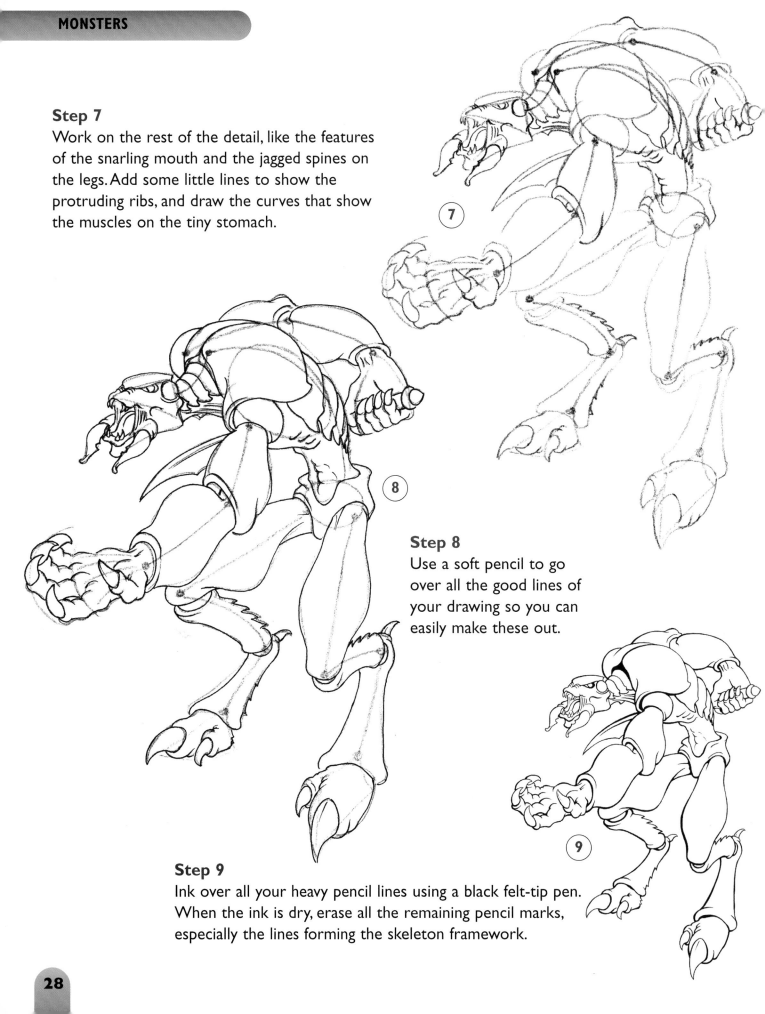

Step 7

Work on the rest of the detail, like the features of the snarling mouth and the jagged spines on the legs. Add some little lines to show the protruding ribs, and draw the curves that show the muscles on the tiny stomach.

Step 8

Use a soft pencil to go over all the good lines of your drawing so you can easily make these out.

Step 9

Ink over all your heavy pencil lines using a black felt-tip pen. When the ink is dry, erase all the remaining pencil marks, especially the lines forming the skeleton framework.

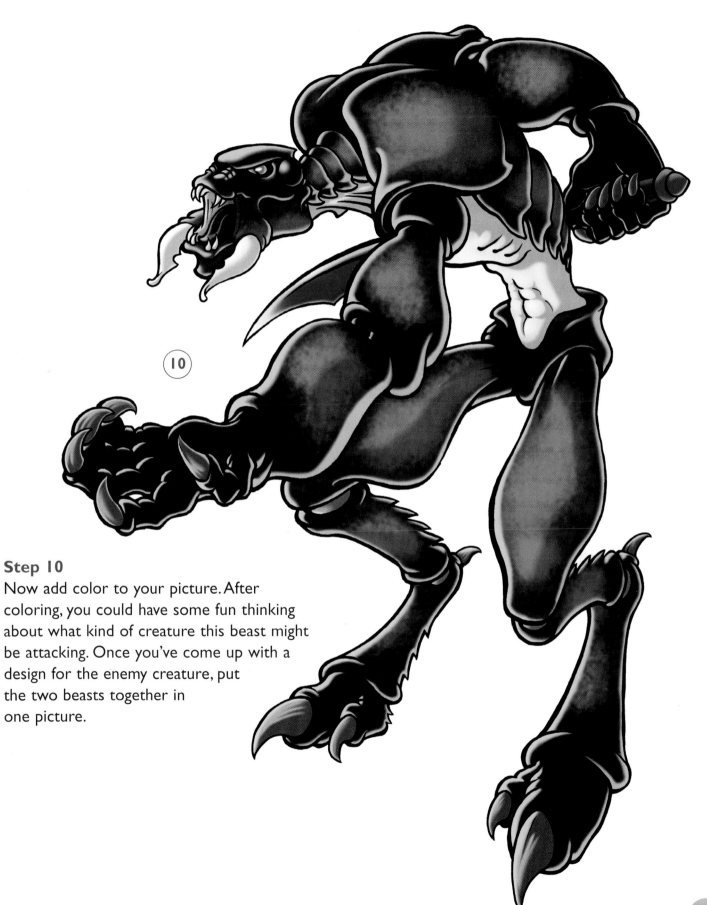

Step 10

Now add color to your picture. After coloring, you could have some fun thinking about what kind of creature this beast might be attacking. Once you've come up with a design for the enemy creature, put the two beasts together in one picture.

Glossary

accentuate (ik-SENT-shuh-wayt) Make more noticeable.

angular (AN-gyuh-lur) Having angles or sharp corners.

anime (A-nih-may) The Japanese word for "animation."

definition (de-fuh-NIH-shun) The clarity of an image.

evolve (ih-VOLV) Develop gradually.

framework (FRAYM-werk) Basic structure.

highlight (HY-lyt) *noun* An area of very light tone in a painting that provides contrast or the appearance of illumination.

highlight (HY-lyt) *verb* Draw attention to something, or make something particularly noticeable.

horizontal (hor-ih-ZON-tul) Parallel to the horizon.

joint (JOYNT) Any of the parts of a body where bones are connected.

manga (MAHN-guh) The literal translation of this word is "irresponsible pictures." Manga is a Japanese style of animation that has been popular since the 1960s.

mutant (MYOO-tent) A creature with an odd or deformed appearance.

proportion (pruh-POR-shun) The relationship between the parts of a whole figure.

protruding (proh-TROOD-ing) Sticking out from the surrounding area.

stance (STANS) The way someone or something stands.

texture (TEKS-chur) The feel or appearance of a surface.

torso (TOR-soh) The upper part of the body, not including head and arms.

vertical (VER-tih-kul) Upright, or at a right angle to the horizon.

watercolor (WA-ter-kuh-ler) Paint made by mixing pigments (substances that give something its color) with water.

Further Information

Books

The Art of Drawing Manga by Ben Krefta (Arcturus, 2003)

How to Draw 101 Monsters (Top That Publishing, 2003)

How to Draw Aliens, Mutants and Mysterious Creatures by Christopher Hart (Watson-Guptill Publications, 2001)

How to Draw Manga: A Step-by-Step Guide by Katy Coope (Scholastic, 2002)

Step-by-Step Manga by Ben Krefta (Scholastic, 2004)

Web Sites

Due to the changing nature of Internet links, PowerKids Press has developed an online list of Web sites related to the subject of this book. This site is updated regularly. Please use this link to access the list: www.powerkidslinks.com/dman/monsters

Index